Mulan

This book is edited and designed by the Editorial Committee of *Cultural China* series.

Story and Illustrations: Li Jian
Translation: Yijin Wert

Copy Editor: Susan Luu Xiang
Editor: Yang Xiaohe
Editorial Director: Zhang Yicong

Senior Consultants: Sun Yong, Wu Ying, Yang Xinci
Managing Director and Publisher: Wang Youbu

ISBN: 978-1-60220-463-8

Address any comments about *Mulan* to:

Better Link Press
99 Park Ave
New York, NY 10016
USA

or

Shanghai Press and Publishing Development Co., Ltd.

F 7 Donghu Road, Shanghai, China (200031)
Email: comments_betterlinkpress@hotmail.com

Printed in China by Shanghai Donnelley Printing Co., Ltd.

1   3   5   7   9   10   8   6   4   2

花木蘭 Mulan

The Story of the Legendary Warrior
Told in English and Chinese

by Li Jian
Translated by Yijin Wert

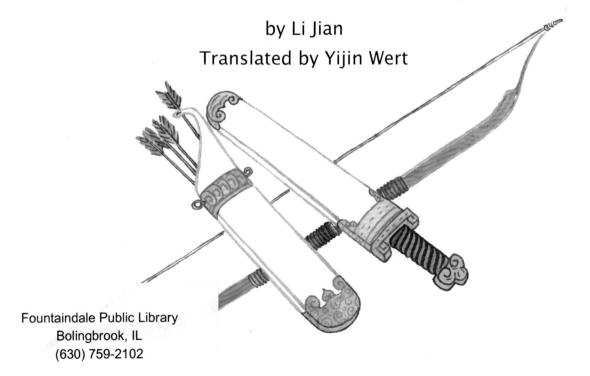

Better Link Press

Mulan learned Chinese calligraphy and reading from her father at a young age. As was the tradition, she also learned weaving and embroidery from her mother.

木兰从小跟着父亲读书写字。作为一项传统，她还跟着母亲学习纺织和刺绣。

Mulan was just as good as the boys at martial arts, but she loved to ride horses and shoot arrows most of all.

木兰还练得一身男儿般的好武艺，但最喜欢骑马和射箭。

One day, an Emperor's messenger delivered a military draft notice to Mulan's father.

一天，衙门里的差役送来了征兵的通知，要征木兰的父亲去当兵。

Mulan's father was too old to fight, and her little brother was too young. How could they possibly go to war? Mulan decided to disguise herself as a man and fulfill her family's duty to protect the country.

父亲老迈，弟弟年幼，他们怎能去杀敌？可是保卫国家的责任又义不容辞，木兰决定女扮男装，代父从军。

Mulan's elder sister and younger brother helped her shop for military supplies, including a spirited horse and a saddle. Now she was ready to set off.

木兰和姐姐、弟弟一起，到集市买好骏马、马鞍和一应所需，准备出发。

Mulan's parents were very sad to see their daughter go, but since they had no other choice, they agreed to let her join the army.

木兰父母虽不舍得女儿出征，但又没有其他办法，只好同意她加入军队。

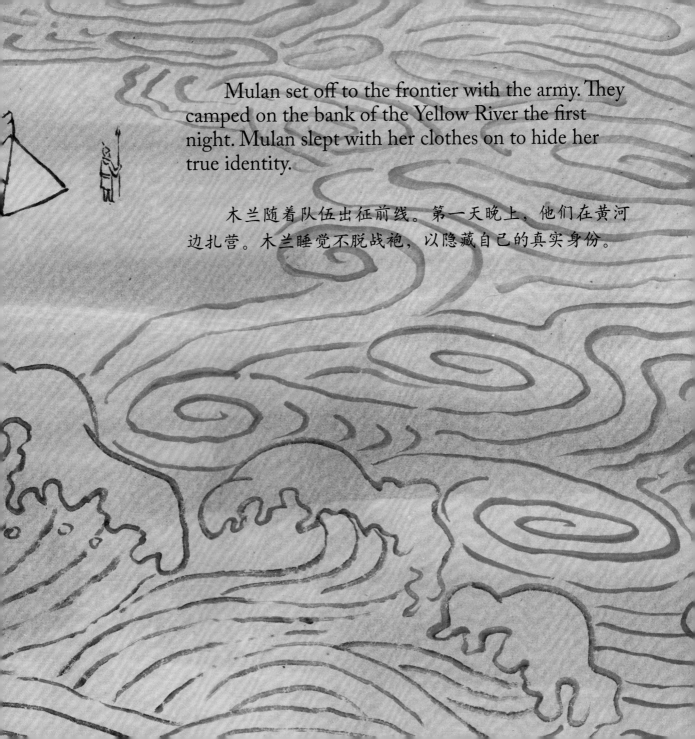

Mulan set off to the frontier with the army. They camped on the bank of the Yellow River the first night. Mulan slept with her clothes on to hide her true identity.

木兰随着队伍出征前线。第一天晚上，他们在黄河边扎营。木兰睡觉不脱战袍，以隐藏自己的真实身份。

The army arrived on the northern mountains the
next day. They heard the sound of their enemy's horses
echoing throughout the mountains.

第二天，队伍抵达了北方的山里，只听见山那边对方
战马的嘶鸣声。

With her skillful martial arts,
Mulan always fought in the front line.

作战的时候，木兰凭着一身好武艺，
冲杀在前。

The war was over.

Mulan distinguished herself again and again during her twelve years of service to the army. She also won the respect of the soldiers who served with her. Everyone praised her for being a brave young man.

战争结束了。

从军十二年，木兰屡建奇功，同伴们对她十分敬佩。

每个人都赞扬她是个勇敢的好男儿。

The Emperor gathered all the heroes together so he could award them for their success. But Mulan refused to accept the official position and declined all the gifts that the Emperor awarded her.

皇帝召见有功的将士，论功行赏。木兰既不想做官，也不想要财物。

She only wished to return home to her family. She asked for a good horse instead, which was immediately granted by the Emperor.

她只希望得到一匹快马，好让她立刻回家。皇帝欣然答应。

Mulan's parents were overjoyed to learn of their daughter's return. They traveled to the very edge of town, waiting to welcome her home.

木兰的父母听说女儿回来欣喜若狂，赶到城外去迎接她回家。

Upon hearing the return of Mulan, her elder sister prepared a grand feast in her honor.

姐姐听说妹妹回来了，在家中准备丰盛的家宴。

Her younger brother cleaned
Mulan's room.

弟弟帮着打扫木兰的房间。

Mulan arrived home. She happily hugged all her family members.

木兰回家了。她高兴地拥抱每一个家人。

Then she took off her warrior's clothes and put on a dress for the first time in many years.

然后，她脱下战袍，换上多年未穿的女装。

Sitting in front of the window, Mulan brushed her hair and put on makeup.

坐在窗前，木兰梳好头，化好妆。

Mulan came out to thank her friends for
bringing her home. Their eyes grew large when
they saw the beautiful Mulan in front of them.

木兰出来向护送她回家的同伴们道谢。当看到美
丽的木兰站在他们面前，同伴们的眼睛瞪得大大的。

Ever since, the story of Mulan has been popular throughout China. It was even made into a poem that has been passed down from generation to generation.

木兰的故事很快就传开了。人们将它编成歌谣，流传至今。

Cultural Explanation

The Ballad of Mulan, also called *The Poem of Mulan*, was a long narrative poem written over 1,500 years ago in China. It has over 300 Chinese characters depicting the wonderful legend of the heroine Mulan, who disguised herself as a man and went to war on her aging father's behalf, and came home in glory.

知识点

《木兰辞》，又称《木兰诗》，是写于1500多年前中国的一首长篇叙事诗，长300余字，描述的是女英雄木兰乔扮男装替父从军、最后光荣还乡的故事，充满传奇色彩。